For Lizzy

When the

Drum Sang

An African Folktale

Written and Illustrated by Anne Rockwell

Parents' Magazine Press • New York

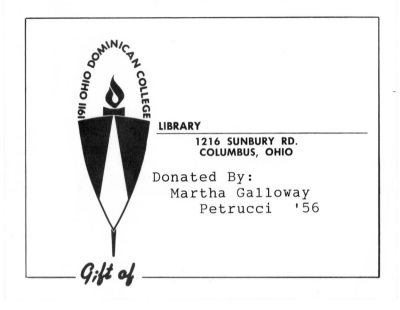
Text and illustrations copyright ©1970 by Anne Rockwell. All rights reserved.
Printed in the United States of America. Library of Congress Catalog card
number: 77-101837. ISBN: Trade 0-8193-0424-7, Library 0-8193-0425-5.

Typography by Jack Jaget

When the Drum Sang

One day a little girl named Tselane went down to the river to fetch water. Dip after dip, she worked to fill her huge gourd calabash, and as she dipped she sang. The song was so beautiful that all of the animals around her, even the crocodile and hippo in the reeds, all stopped whatever they were doing and listened to the little girl sing.

In the tall grass, not far from her, a man with a drum sat and listened too. Now if he had been a good man, he would have listened quietly and then gone away. But he was *not* a good man, but a very bad *zimwe*, and so a bad idea came into his head. Just as Tselane had almost filled her calabash with water, the man sneaked up behind her as she sang and thrust her into his drum, which was bigger than she was.

Before she could cry out, the man said to her, "Little girl, you sing well. Now, listen to me. When I beat this drum, you must sing, as well and as long as you can. If you do not sing, I will beat *you* instead of my drum!"

Tselane was frightened, and so she told him she would do what he said. So the man took his big drum with the little girl inside and went away.

When he came to a village some miles away, it was nearly evening, and he stopped by the village and asked if he might spend the night. The chief answered that he could, and so the man said that he wished to play the drum for all the people to thank them for their hospitality.

"Boom! Boom!" He beat the drum and Tselane began to sing. She sang and sang and all of the villagers listened happily to the beautiful music.

When she stopped they all cried out, "Please, stranger, play your singing drum again!"

But the man answered, "I am hungry and tired, and I cannot play my drum until I eat."

When the people heard this they hurried to their gardens and filled their baskets with all the good things they could find to eat. There were big golden pumpkins, and fat yams, and red beans, and bananas. These they cooked and brought to the man, along with fresh goat's milk and sweet honey-beer. He ate and ate and drank and drank until all the good things were gone. Then—"Boom! Boom!"—he beat the drum and Tselane began to sing, and she sang and sang and sang until the moon was high in the sky. Then she sang lullabies and did not stop until all of the villagers were nodding their heads sleepily.

Then, when everyone had gone to bed, the man opened up the top of the drum and gave the little girl five small cold beans that were all that was left of his big dinner, even though she was quite hungry after so much singing.

When morning came, the man went away, taking his wonderful drum, and went on to another village. The same thing happened as the night before, but this time the people even cooked him a chicken stew which he gobbled up, saving none at all for Tselane. From village to village he went, and wherever he went, it was always the same. No one had ever heard such beautiful sounds as came from the singing drum, and so wherever he went people feasted him with all the good things they could find.

But did he share any of this with poor little Tselane, locked in the dark drum? No, he did not; he only gave her enough to keep her voice from growing small and weak . . . four or five cold beans, or a few pumpkin seeds.

When Tselane had not returned to her village her mother and father had gone to the river to look for her. Not a sign of her did they see—except her big calabash, nearly filled with water. Along the river's edge a crocodile blinked at them, and they asked him if he had eaten their little girl, but he shook his head and swam away.

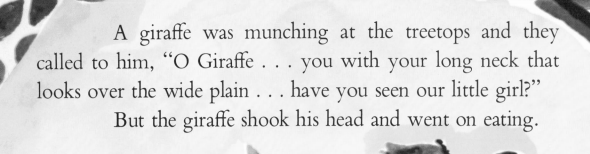

A giraffe was munching at the treetops and they called to him, "O Giraffe . . . you with your long neck that looks over the wide plain . . . have you seen our little girl?"

But the giraffe shook his head and went on eating.

They called to a lion in the grass, "Where is our little girl—Tselane who sings so sweetly? Have you eaten her?"

But the lion shook his mane and ran away.

On and on the mother and father wandered until they met an elephant.

"O Elephant . . . with your great ears . . . have you heard news of our little lost girl?"

But the elephant shook his head sadly, and slowly ambled away.

Then they met a hyena, an ugly, unpleasant fellow.

"Hyena, please, do you know where our little girl— Tselane who sings so sweetly—where might she be?"

But the hyena only laughed a nasty, sneering laugh and slunk away.

For weeks and weeks Tselane's mother and father wandered, always asking for their little girl, but no one had seen or heard of her. They grew dusty and ragged from their journeying from forest to plain, from village to village, but their little girl was not to be found.

One evening, tired and hungry, they stopped at a village and asked to spend the night. The villagers welcomed them and told them that there was another stranger staying in the village that night, but there was still room for more. The other stranger was the man with the drum that sang.

"Boom! Boom!"—he beat the drum and it began to sing.

Tselane, hidden inside, sang songs about the beautiful things she had known when she lived outside the drum in the bright sunshine . . . about little antelopes running through the tall grass . . . about the gentle bleating of newborn baby kids, and about blue mountains reaching for the sky.

Because she was sure she would never see these things again she sang sad songs about happy things, and they were lovelier than any songs she had ever before sung. All the people held their breath so as not to miss a note.

Except one. No sooner had Tselane begun to sing when her mother, sitting close to the drummer, started to cry out for she recognized the voice of her dear little girl. But her father looked sternly at his wife, and so she said nothing, but instead sat very still and listened. For hours and hours the drum sang, and each song was more beautiful than the one before.

When the singing was done—for at last the man said he could play no longer unless he was fed—all of the people brought him the best foods they had, and he ate and ate and ate.

"I am thirsty!" he cried out when he had eaten enough for ten men, and then the people brought him calabashes and ostrich-egg cups of sweet honey-beer, and he drank and drank and drank, while Tselane's father sat near him and flattered him about his wonderful drum and urged him to eat and drink some more.

At last, when he had drunk enough for twenty men, he gave a great yawn, and fell asleep. All the people in the village went to their houses to sleep, but Tselane's parents only pretended to sleep. When they were sure that everyone was asleep and the drummer was snoring louder than a lion, they crept up to him. Quietly, quietly, they untied the thongs that held the drum skin to the drum and peeped inside. There was their little girl, small and thin and frightened and lonely.

"Come out, come out," they whispered to her and held her tight.

Then her father took a little fire on a stick and crept out into the forest.

Near an old tree he held the stick of fire, and after a moment many, many bees came out of a hole in the tree, for they did not like the smoke from the man's fire.

As they swarmed around not knowing where to go, the man put the stick close to them and they flew ahead of him to escape the smoke. In this way he drove them on ahead of him and right back to the village of sleeping people, and up to the man's empty drum.

Seeing the nice hole in the drum, quite like a hole in a dead tree, the bees all flew in, and the father snapped the drum skin over the drum and smiled.

Then the family went to sleep.

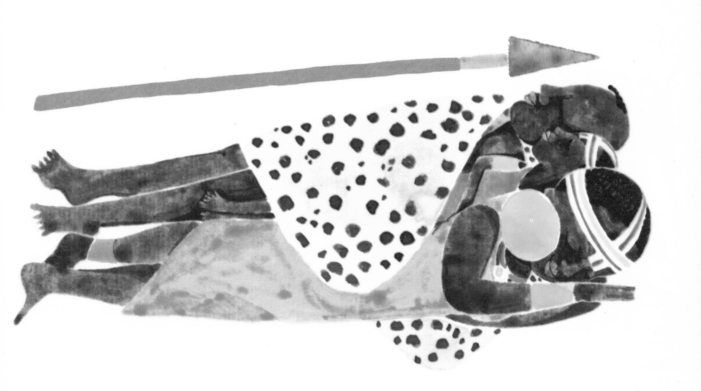

Morning came, and when everyone awoke they begged the man to play his drum again. No one noticed the strange little girl who was there, for they talked of nothing but the beautiful songs of the drum.

"Please, please," they begged the man over and over again. "Play the drum for us again before you go."

And the man rubbed his stomach and said, "I could play the drum quite well, if I only had a little breakfast!"

And the people then promised him that they would feast him with even more food than the night before, and would give him many presents besides, if he would only play one little short song before they went into their gardens to pick a feast for him—for there was nothing left in their houses.

And so the man agreed: one little song, that was all.

"Boom! Boom!"—he beat the drum, but nothing happened.

"Boom! Boom! BOOM!"—angrily he beat the drum again.

Nothing happened and a few people began to laugh at him.

"BOOM! BOOM! BOOM! BOOM! BOOM! . . . BOOM! BOOM! BOOM!" Again and again he beat the drum, but nothing happened . . . nothing at all. By now all of the people were laughing and laughing at him. Then he threw his drum on the ground, and kicked it and shouted at it, but still the drum was silent.

At last, he picked up the drum and ran angrily out of the village, shouting to the drum, "I told you I would beat you if you did not sing—and now I *will!*"

So saying, he tore off the drum skin to beat Tselane, but—Oh my!

Out came the bees . . . so many of them!
"Bzzzzzzzzzzzzzzz . . . zzzzzzzzz . . ." and they flew after that man and chased him away, and no one ever saw or heard of him again.

As for Tselane, she sang a beautiful happy song for the people before they went back to their gardens to work, and so everyone gave her good things to eat (for she was very hungry after being in the drum so long), and a pretty necklace besides. Then she and her mother and father began their journey home.

A NOTE ABOUT THE STORY

Among the Bantu peoples of southern Africa there are many stories of a special kind of gluttonous ogre called a *zimwi*. This is one of the most widely told *zimwi* tales and it appears among many different tribes in different versions. Unlike many African folktales which are told for religious or instructive purposes, stories of the imaginary *zimwi* are told purely for the amusement and entertainment of the listener, young and old. A *zimwi* can take many forms and resort to many tricks to satisfy his enormous appetite; sometimes he is a giant; sometimes he has but one leg; occasionally he disguises himself as a hyena, the most disliked African beast; and sometimes he, like the *zimwi* in the story, pretends to be a rather ordinary person—but greedier than most!